THE
COMING
AGE
AND OTHER
POEMS

THE
COMING
AGE
AND OTHER
POEMS

JAMES W. CUMMINGS

ARPress
ILLUMINATING IDEAS.
EMPOWERING VOICES

ARPress
45 Dan Road Suite 5
Canton MA 02021
Hotline: 1(888) 821-0229
Fax: 1(508) 545-7580

Ordering Information:

Quantity sales. Special discounts are available on quantity purchases by corporations, associations, and others. For details, contact the publisher at the address above.

Printed in the United States of America.

ISBN-13:   Softcover   979-8-89330-747-4

                eBook   979-8-89330-748-1

Library of Congress Control Number: 2024902884

Table Of Contents

THE CANDLE REVISITED

Some People have wondered where I got my gift for poetry
Since I started, I have learned It was on both sides of the family tree
Mom's Aunt Hazel wrote beautifully, Gram's Aunt Sadie too
Verses One could read and visualize the view
My "Light" was ignited way back when I was five
In the McKinley school past which remains One still may drive
Jake Gould bought it, moved it down by the corner and made it a garage
Another little Photo in History's collage
My brother Ron had a poem about a candle He was supposed to recite
How He struggled with that but couldn't seem to get it right
At the Rehearsal for the Christmas pageant, I stood by his side
As He stumbled through it I did something no one should have to abide
I opened my yap and proudly spoke the words
About a Candle in a window somewhere in the world
Ron got another poem to read to the classes
The Grownups who were there and the lads and lasses

THE COMING AGE

Days of Change are Coming, what does the future hold
New Ways will come to us and sweep aside the old
Always Things are like this yet occasionally reverse
Things may come back to us after in the new we have ourselves immersed
There will be Edsels and Tuckers in the coming age
Inventions not up to snuff or the public not ready for at this stage
Some will be harmful and so discontinued
Others cast aside as we ever find new venues
The Internet is changing, offer more info and security.
Yet Continue in a Form, that is a surety
Birth defects will be quelled until perhaps they no longer exist
We`ll come close to conquering disease and age yet some will likely persist
Aqua culture will thrive in this era
Population could be a challenge and growth of food for all
Explorations into Space may either boom or stall
Days of Change are here, we enter a new Era
We pray to God that life as a whole will be fairer

RELATIVE HUNTING

It's an odd and fascinating thing to trace One's relatives
Immigrants, recent or long agone or American Natives!
They claim that even the last were immigrants though who can say for
sure that That was wholy true, now I'll say no more
After a few Generations No one can prove a pedigree without DNA
Say what you may
There's no more scientific way to prove who did roll who, in the hay
Still, it's an enormous achievement to find documented lines way
Back which say so and so was such and such's child
Despite All I've said against it, it's interesting to discover that that
Rowdy's father was a man meek and mild
The Rich Men, the Poor Men, the Beggars and Thieves
The Doctor, the King, the Bootlegger and the whomever else lies
among the roots
The Valiant, the Coward, those Noble by the birth or deed
Patriots, Loyalist, Liar, Honest Men, Slaves, Person of All Stripe and
Creed
Blood is thicker that water, it's often said and true
It's a tangled Web of Ancestors and who knows you might get right
somehow
As He stumbled through it I did something no one

MOTHERS MAKE THE WORLD

It's Mothers who first make the World a wondrous place
Even more so in this Age with its' frantic pace
Mothers heal usually and take too much guff
Every Mother has a softness, even those who are tough
They wait and hope their children do grow up
Sometimes Having to speed the process up
Mothers teach lessons, first are sacrifice and Love
Keys that can gain Us entry into Heaven above
Mothers carry life with a little inconstant help
They teach mercy, that Babies make a heart melt
Mothers teach Us manners and the essence of the Word
But before all else, Mothers make the World

A SOLDIER

A Soldier stood erect shoulders straight with pride
In a Line with Others standing there beside
A Soldier knelt behind the sandbags awaiting enemies
With the fellow Soldiers striving to make a country free
A Soldier sat in a cockpit in mid-air
Below Trying to ascertain what went on there
A Soldier worked to rebuild when destruction was done
Doing what was necessary for the good of everyone
A Soldier wept for the fallen, the others who had died
The harsh Reality of the price sometimes paid by those try
A Soldier stood risking all for what Fate might decide
For Them and the others who stood there beside

A Sidney Family: Eleazer Cummings III

Eleazer Cummings` father died shortly after his birth
His Mother Martha Browne raised him after his father Eleazer left this earth
Brother Samuel moved to Dracut and was wounded at Bunker Hil
Eleazer ended up in Sandy River there to plant and till
He wed Anna Ward in Vassalborough , daughter of John of that town
They lived near there and in the area some descendants can still be found
Anna`s sister Mindwell married Lemuel Jackson, a Baptist preacher
Lemuel`s brother- In- law Asa Wilbur was a local reverend and teacher
Eleazer in the years that followed property in Sidney did acquire
He and Anna had ten children all they could desire
They grew prosperous but experienced grief
When their son William died in New York during the War of Eighteen twelve
Before the year Eighteen Thirteen passed Eleazer died himself
In the Army in NewYork He too fought the British dying in the war
His Wife Anna would survive for twenty - six years more.

Joseph S Cummings of Belgrade Maine

Joseph was a prosperous man in Sidney and Belgrade town
Ann Prescott his wife had Kin of great renown
This Cummings was a farmer whose sons did go to college
He had interest in a railroad this I do acknowledge
Joseph was a righteous man who saw Heaven's light
At three Baptist churches He prayed with all his might
Were Piety and prosperity related; interesting speculation
It was much the same for several of his Relations
Five Sons and five daughters survived to maturity
Marriage and children were ahead for the Majority
A Selectman in Belgrade, Joseph was well respected there
He raised cattle, sheep, stallions and mares

Brooks, Maine Field Day Derby - July 2005

It was a different Year, the Field was small
The Show was big, held all in thrall
Brooks Field Day, July Two Thousand and Five
There should be more Entries there when October arrives
Larry and Lois Lainey come clown from Sebec
Like every Year, Hard hitting Drivers who give and receive some good natured heck
Gene Stetson and Bub Shorey were also in the field that summer day
To Participate in the Fireworks the Independence Day way
Todd from Knox was there too
Giving a good show in a car of blue
Charlie Cummings was there with sister Maria Kingsbury, both of Dixmont town
Drove Station wagons 1776 and 21 to Victory, for Charlie second, for Maria the crown
A magnificent Trophy, all red, white and blue
Some Money besides for both It was true
Proud Mother Marjorie and I watched from beside the rope in chairs of green
Both Plan to return with their Cars in October, whatever that outcome will be

Terror

On the eleventh of September in the year two thousand one
A war broke out, without a gun
Upon that day our world went insane
Things in our nation shall never be the same
Two gleaming towers that New York stood
Ceased to exist suddenly as none thought they could
Terrorist controlled planes hit them head on
Creating the beginning of one of the darkest days the sun has shone
on
Another hit the Pentagon in another action nobody should defend
Or between the two, Thousands of innocents wound up dead
Who knows who ordered this grievous of attacks
Ben laden, Saddam, or another should their head lack
May the guilty soon be punished without a place to go
been stomping out all terror, this world has been too slow.

A Death in Loudon

Losing someone is always hard, no matter how prepared we are
Yet the sudden ending of a life is more horrible by far
Stock car racing is a dangerous sport, but seldom are the crashes life's end
Recently a young man of much promise died, one whom many called friend
At Loudon in New Hampshire, Adam Petty ran his final race
Just as beside his family he was starting to take his place
He ran one race in Winston Cup earlier this year
No one dreamed what would happen, nobody was a seer
His grandfather Richard survived many crashes by God's good will alone
The Lord but recently called great grandfather Lee to stand beside his throne
That's all we ever have, the trick of fate or whim of God
Now Adam has joined Lee lo stand before the Lord

The King (Richard Lee Petty)

He started back when Nextel was but a tiny pup
Long before most People had a clue anything was up
His father, Lee had great success as did Junior and Fireball
They won plenty of races years before anyone had heard of malls
In an age of "'Innocence" when tobacco was not a sin
There came a tall, spare young Man with a big old Pepsodent grin
He was talkative and amiable, winning fans for this 'new' sport
Aiming for this Franchise's Drivers sponsors of a more profitable sort
He won a bunch of races, though the competition was tough
Among Him, Pearson, Bobby Allison and Yarborough things sometimes got rough
The years passed, He won more races, his wife Linda by his side
Watching as He won or sometimes had rough rides
later Bobby Allison retired, and younger drivers came to the fore
Daviell Allison, Bill Elliot and Dale Earnhardt to name a few there were many more
His son Kyle started racing, Tim Richmond, and Dale Jarrell too
The wins came not so often now, yet He still had a few
Two hundreds wins in Nextel Cup Richard had before He retired
More than any Other in his Division, in this I am no liar
All in All, this Ride to fame was quite something
So, say "Hey" Richard Petty, Nextel's one and only king

Working in the Woods

The Buzz of Chainsaws fills the air
Trees are falling so try to take care
Lest Accident befall you and keep you away from work
You must keep real alert, or you may come to hurt
Yet Alertness and care alone won't protect you
Tree felling is a risky business no matter how you hew
But it is necessary to keep some of the land clear
New Trees spring up with every passing year
If You don't at least cut bushes in your fields They'll overgrow
Burning Wood wards off some chill of winter snows
Firewood and paper are big industries in Maine
Very Likely, that They shall remain

The Road

Along the Road I walk and along it the wonders of the world do see
The Beauties of Nature along with some Man wanted to be
Oaks and Elms whose branches almost seem to brush the skies
Bushes growing inside rocks that seem to the laws of nature defy
A big old rambling House that has seen generations come and go
It looks as though it may withstand another one or so
Perhaps We should consider where the stream runs through
Where People go out in boots or boats to try to fish whether the sky
is gray or blue
Then there is that old Building up the road that always looks like
it's about to fall down
But There's almost always Somewhere like that in Everyone's
Home town
Even in the City where the roads are streets
Where Buildings are mostly built of brick and concrete
Someplace there is Something like all I've told about
No matter the number of elegant Places the critics tout

Cycle

Beginning, end, it's all but one
Turn but once a season's done
Turn but twice a Year half gone
Turn three times It's come the fall
Turn You four then again it's all
So swift Time goes from year-to-year
Unhindered Alike by sorrow and cheer
Beginning, end it's all but one
Before You know it a life is done

On the Field of Flodden

The King gave Arran command of 'Great Michael'
which I le shouldn't have done
He accepted Surrey's challenge of mistakes his second one
Arran, the crazy fool raided English ships, in judgment He did lack
As the Ship 'Great Michael' was supposed to be protecting our back
The morning Fog and mournful skirl of pipes did presage our gloom
As we marched out on Flodden Field there to meet our certain doom
Montrose led our left flank, the King the center and Lennox led the
right
Though our Women will weep and wail,
Some English women will do the same tonight
The King fell earlier in the afternoon
Pierced and Hacked on all sides, be it up to the English,
He'll not have a tomb
Chiefs and clansmen lay about, their bodies are quite gory
Scarce a One remains alive, this day has no glory
Across The Bodies lay tattered banners with many a device
The King should have listened to the Earl of Angus' advice
My Sword slips from my fingers and I fall upon my knees
Soon Now, I reckon I shall cease to breathe
"Ah King Jamie wha hae ye done" I ask in my final breath
"A wee Bairn is Scotland's king now ye lie in death"

Master of the Vessel

Fair blows the Wind that fills my sail
I make good time now, yet I know It soon should fail I'm off to Jamaica
for rum and molasses
I'll stop there some days so my lads can woo comely lasses
Master am I of all I behold
Whoe'er says else I'll cast in the hold
I deal full sternly with any malcontent
Yet I'm not so unreasonable that I cause dissent
Aye, I' m known for a full hard driving man
I can make the hardiest blanch beneath his tan
All know this, else soon do find out
When I must I'll cut their backs to ribbons so They've no cause to
doubt
We'll unload the rum in New York sooner than some might wish
Then We'll set sail for Boston to get a load of fish
The Sea's a harsh Mistress to We seamen no matter how bold
I'm a harsh Master when Men don't do as They're told
So raise Ye the sails and head into the wind
That We might the sooner be home in Portland again

A Place Called Sand Creek

I'll tell you now a story about barbarity at its' peak
About how a Troop of US Calvary conducted itself at Sand Creek
Murder and Multilation were the order on that day
"Kill All, for Nits make lice" Colonel Chivington did say
Mack Kettle's white flag was ignored, even as his shout
Chivington had it perfect, the fighting men were out
So He and his men so valiant did kill the ferocious squaws and their papoose
They probably won a commendation, but They all deserved a noose
Save for the few Soldiers who refused to participate, made themselves the odd man out
Or Worse, helped the dread enemy so
They hey were thought a traitorous lout
Mack Kettle led some women and children in escape, great villain that He was
Those Cheyennes were not on the reservation
So the Government thought the Calvary had sufficient cause
'Hostiles' They were designated so any conduct went
Even such atrocities as this disgruntled soldier could give vent How Ironic that a man call himself civilized and treat another as a beast
Yet, That's generally what Civilization has ever been like
From the West to Far East

Everyone Is Special

Sometimes People ask me "How do you write poems so fast?"
Well, I wonder about that too but it's nice of you to ask
You see, it's not difficult for me to see a different view
I get ideas not just from me but from other people too
It's not Mystical nor magical to have this certain knack
I use words to try and make up for some skills that I lack
Everyone's a wizard when it comes to certain things
There are those who seemingly can do anything at all
Painters, Writers, Poets, people in all the Arts
'Ordinary" People who have all kinds of smarts
Carpenters, Plumbers and Masons who don't get credit enough
Repairmen and Electricians, manufacturers of all sorts of stuff
Everyone is Special in their special way
From Doctors curing people to farmers curing hay

A Win at Martinsville

At Martinsville in West Virginia NASCAR runs a couple races
In October Two Thousand One the Winner brought a smile to many
a face
Ricky Craven grew up in Newburgh deep in the heart of Maine
After Years of trying and contending, He got to Victory lane
He lead nearly a fifth of the laps, itself no small feat
With Harvick, and Jarrett near it could easily become a defeat
Jarrett nearly passed Him on the final lap
Like Many other Drivers, Ricky kept him back with a tap
Ricky Craven has a heart as big as Maine's North woods
Now He has got a big reward; He showed the world He could

Darlington, March 2003

Who can forget the race at Darlington this season
Such a close Finish would be the reason
Kurt Busch was leading and held on tight
Craven came forward and battled with all his might
Two Cars became as One so close did They strive
Mere Inches separated them when the finish arrived
Dave Blaney came in third and might have won the race
But Fate intended otherwise in that time and place
Two great and lucky Drivers took first and second at that time
That's what Crowds come to see, a finish cut so fine
Busch nearly held fast to his lead that day
Fate and Luck granted Ricky Craven his second they say

Christmas Unicorn

Of all God's Creatures great and small
It's claimed He loved the Unicorn best of all
So like a Horse but with a horn in his forehead
Yet pristine White mirroring purity when all is done and said
A gentle, peaceful Beast to no vice inclined
Innocent as an Angel; Humor far better than mine
These magical beloved Creatures long since have been gone
Perhaps only in Imagination do Unicorns belong
With the Griffin and the Dragon, steeped in myth and mystery
Exploding upon the Silver Screen of dream and fantasy
Where Good and Evil do collide and Good wins in the end
Against Incredible Odds with useful aid from good friends
Now We make them out of plastic, porcelain or glass
Figurines of legendary animals beloved of every class
Peace, Love and Beauty Unicorns embody for all time
The single perfect Animal to celebrate Christmas time

The Lighthouse

It stood upon a crag silhouetted against the autumn evening sky
It's only movement came from it's wandering fiery eyes
It stood above sharply jutting rocks
amid crashing waves and boiling spray
Many believed it had seen better days
Beside a ruined house where families had stayed
Who kept things in good condition and the light ablaze
A harbinger of hope to seamen through the years
A sight to gladden hearts and bring them cheer
Today it's decommissioned, another part of history
Tourists come from faraway to hear it's okay
Locals point to it and exclaim in disgust or pride
Dependent on their view when the subject does arise

Time of Despair

Too young, lost, lonely and scared
Wondering why she was so stupid on that night they shared
Future looking gloomy, dark and dim
Why had she given herself so completely to him?
Too young - desperately hoping things turn out right
Why hadn't he gotten protection to use that night?
Dumb kids - too anxious for a thrill
But the deed being done, he stands behind her still
He was told by his buddies:
'No one will blame you much if you back away'
Her friends tell her to abort her child, that he will never stay
Sometimes she's not even sure she wants him to
He's not mean and abusive, but he seems way too blue
Their lives changed within a heartbeat,
Dimness where once the future seemed bright
But it's too late, even if she followed her friend's
Advice nothing will be all right.

Caliburn

Sword of power, sword of might
Sword of honor, sword of right
Ensorcelled sword of all the ages
Powerful in all your many stages
Forged by dwarves of mayhap God
He who wields you in ever Lord
I drew you forth from the rock because Kay's was lost
Drew you forth despite the ice and frost
I drew you forth again when the earth was reborn
Then Merlin told me for what purpose I had been born
To make prosper this land now so lean
I doubt I have the wisdom to do if, I'm just fifteen
I drew you forth and crown and land I earned
May I ever wield you in justice, my sword my Caliburn

A Scabbard and Camelot

Five Years have passed since to pull the sword from the stone I strove
Then did Merlin take Caliburn to the lake and with it's Lady magic
wove
Now I aspire to wed a comely princess of grace
She is Gwenyfar of Camelot, daughter of Leodegrace
I am grown to manhood with skill and might in arms
Grown cleverer in Council and albeit in courtly charms
I broke my sword in battle and was wounded sore
Merlin took me to the lake and to me the sword Caliburn restored
He gave it back to me in a scabbard of plain but polished wood
On a plain black leathern belt I liked not as I should
Thus I told Merlin when He asked and He called me a fool
He said for my success the scabbard was ten times the tool
For whene'er I do wear it never shall I come to hurt
Not by Sword nor sling, nor arrow, not by lance nor sharpened dirk
Thus I did try it out and unfairly won the day
No did Merlin tell me when I returned from the fray
My Wedding Day is set, Word spread the land around
When I wed Gwenyfar at Camelot Merlin shall make for me a table
round
I am to receive only Knights of noblest purpose and mind
All to sit in equality with all other I do find.

In Memoriam

Like Cordwood stored the corpses lie
Honored Soldiers side by side
From the sick Tent pain and death
Evidence of Battle and loss of health
Too Young, but not too young to die
Did as told without asking why
Who knows who lost or won
Many never saw another sun
Crecy, Somalia, Hastings, Algiers
Same as each other in different years
We honor all who gave up all
For misguided Glory did They fall
Rusted Weaponry, Helmets split
'Fields of Honor' littered by such as this
The Young, the Old, the Cautious, the Proud
Fought each Other in battle loud
Land, Money and Thought
The Reasons these Wars were fought
Never will there be a moratorium
We Recall these Men only in memoriam

A Town in Maine

As the Sun sets I glance off toward purple shadowed hills
My Heart with wonder at such majesty fills
It is a fairly quiet Town and therein lies its' charm
Though even now the Crowding in some areas gives me an alarm
Land of Several of my fathers that you are are indeed
I must wait and see where the future does us lead
Change must come to us even as the seasons do
We can only hope and pray that not too much will We rue
As I walk upon this road past old familiar haunts
I wonder what will be in the Town of Dixmont

The Coming Dawn

What will We see in the coming dawn?
That We didn't see the last date the sun gazed on
Today brings new beginnings, fresh possibilities
For Everyone to improve, all utilizing their best abilities
Construction, Destruction both lie in our hands
Everywhere from forests to cities to burning sands
We have reasons to worry yet also to hope
Just do what We can and don't bother to mope
We need not be weak and scurry along
Nor need We stand alone to appear strong
Pride's a pricey folly in times such as these
We must protect and preserve Everyone's needs
Be Vigilant yet fair in our deeds
Look not on Things with a mind too narrow
We can't afford to be too shallow
We must stand strong, be firm in All We can
This Year prove Ourselves the better women and men

The Pumpkin Man: - Jack O' Lantern

Once upon the Night of the Pumpkin Ball
Into the wood strode a Man, He was quite tall
With hair as dark as a raven's wing
He cared only for himself of everything
A Cottage he spied near the forest track
No one was near neither front nor back
Jack (so He was called) decided for his part
That He would go inside and found there - pumpkin tarts
He set down his lantern which He carried aloft
He bit the warm pastries, so gooey and soft
He had another, then two and then three
He had five more, then six - so went his spree
He gobbled not caring whose vittles He ate
As his love for those Tarts he tried to sate
The Goblin whose cottage had been invaded appeared
He had come to get his tarts, the ball's time was drawing near
He had so promised his fellow goblins, witches, trolls and sprites
Who had All gathered for their annual Ball upon this night
Jack of the Lantern had been foolish to tick this goblin off
"A Pumpkin Head ever will you be" He shrieked, quite cross
No Jack became a monstrosity for all eternity
The Lantern gleams within for Everyone to see
Thus his selfishness did cost him the semblance of life
All in account of the pumpkin tarts He chose to kief

Jacquetta

Ten Score of years had passed for Jack
Since that Goblin laid that curse upon his back
His Pumpkin Head did not spoil nor fire in it burn
Though every Year to the next did turn
Lonely Jack had been possessing all memory of the man
Recalling all that had befallen him back within time's sands
He caught the eye of a lovely Witch, Jacquetta was her name
She had sky blue eyes and raven hair and hoped He felt the same
"Would You ask me to dance" She asked her voice soft and low
Jack declined the honor saying: "I couldn't be your fellow"
Jacquetta blinked, then nodded and uttered words passing strange
Before Jack Pumpkinman's eyes She began to change
Jacquetta's comely face grew round and orange as was his
The Witch's lips shrank, drew back and became a carven grin
Jack stared anew at Jacquetta and took her hand to dance
The Witch got what She wanted by taking a simple chance
From then to Eternity always One is with the other
By Going to such lengths Jacquetta proved
She would never love another

The Pumpkin Ball

The Clock's at eleven They all have come here
There's Jack and Jacquetta like every year
This Party's attended by every Golem, Goblin and Ghoul
Wizards and witches They all think They're cool
This Monster's Bash comes but once a year
Dracula's clan and the Werewolves all are here
Pumpkin Ale and Tarts and other favorite treats
Did Anyone Anyone remember what Pharoah Wepwethotep likes to eat
Honeyed Dates and Locusts too all is good
In this House in the middle of the wood
There is music, the Monsters dance
In the stately Waltz All did prance
Midnight strikes, All Saints shall come
The Monsters will prepare to fight, Everyone
The Angels cast them down again
Balance returns to this World We're in

Enduring Love

We've been togcther many years through both trial and error
We raised our children, but they could be terrors
Now They're gone and married and some of their children as well
But I only need to breathe for love in my heart still to swell
Though They're all grown they do worry us sometimes still
But Somehow We'll get over life's next hill
Like an Oak, Love's roots are strong and long can It endure
Through wherever destiny leads us to what the future holds in store

The Surfer

He was born amid the waves some time agone
Child of the surf, the place He belongs
Give Him a board and shorts, He's out to sea
Someplace between Vieux Boucau and Wakiki
There's Wahinis better than most dudes out in the surf
Gone are the Days when It was just a Dude's turf
He's wherever the big waves crash from Malibu to Japan
On the Gold Coast, New Zealand They're near most every land
He has been to places where tourists almost never go
Those wild untamed Gems of surf that very few do know
Sure, He still surfs Pipe, enters the contests too
To Make enough money to do what he loves to do
Time was People like him went from this job to that
Rootless, drifting to where the good Surf was at
Now There's serious Money in this as in other sports
So serious some places have special Surf reports

One Landmark Christmas

Tucked away in the corner of our minds
We all have favorite memories
Those special if somewhat brief times of menorah or Christmas trees
A thoughtful Gift of large or small price paid
That gave Joy to your heart which a while stayed
A tiny fabric Doll made by a Mother's hands
A Guitar, Trumpet or Drum for someone to get into a band
A carefully cut and pasted card a Child gave a Parent
Maybe a favorite Pet, a puppy or a parrot
A standing Warrior molded in dance for some Indian 'nut'
Most Things there but briefly before they somehow went kaput
We are so careless of material, especially when young
Ending with these memories and not the things We gained them from

The Wizard's Pupil

Mika was a boy who lived in a magical land
Fortunate enough to have a wizard take him in hand
Justus, his master was steeped in arcane lore
Mika wasn't grateful, merely thought his teacher a bore
He longed to cast powerful spells though not yet a teen
Justus laid down strict rules on which Mika wasn't keen
One Day the Wizard went out leaving half made brew
He ordered the boy to stir the pot, adding not, orders Mika did eschew
Hc added wolfsbane and a little eye of newt
He ladled some up and spilled it on his boot
There was a bang, Mika was nowhere to be seen
A big fat Toad sat on the pupil's clothes, ah, but fate was mean
Justus returned saw this toad and turned it back into the boy shaking
his head to and fro
By the Powers that are, this strange m'Boy, how painful it is to grow

Mika and the Dragon`s Claws

This Impetuous boy, Mika of that distant magic place
Fooled with another potion, disappeared without a trace
Justus heard his breathing determined the fix he was in
The Wizard was less than sympathetic and told the boy`s kin
He`d have no more to do with him nor even help him in his plight
Unless Mika brought him the claws of a dragon for a brew to restore
him to others` sight
Mika howled and bellowed he was so sore afraid
He had no wish to enter the cave wherein the dragon laid
Justus gave Mika his magic blade and bade him clip the dragon`s
claws
The Youth entered the cave though frightened at what he saw
The Dragon lay in slumber near the rear cave wall
Mika started clipping claws the dragon minded not at all

The Boy gathered up the claws and took them to the mage
Justus made the potion and restored Mika back to average

Di

A Lady from the House of Spencer she chisr to wed a Prince
For Love more than title She tried herself to convince
Prince Charles may of wed her for her bloodlines, that elder Stuart stock
For in his veins, of Charles II oe James II there flows nary a drop
Diana possessed that common touch even as Charles II of long ago
That made the People love her the better to want to know
While not quite innocent herself her Prince was a cad who loved another more
She likely soon knew what lie in store
Charles was too public with his mistress and brought his young wife grief
Though sad in a way, Divorce must have brought Di a degree of relief
Mother of a future King her place cannot be denied
Nor Her warmth to common folk in Heaven She resides
Too Young to die , Yet God called her from those she loved
She shall long be remembered by us in that land above

Veteran

The wild eyed panic of Youth has become a steely calm
Fingers twitching on the trigger seeking safety from harm
With that comes the Knowledge that harm shall likely come
With so many Opponents you likely won`t see where all comes from
Not Bullets nor grenades else so many little bombs
They do so much damage wearing down the strong
It`s been a mad and terrible world so many getting killed
Your Addrenalin`s pumping so hard , One who didn`t know might
thing you thrilled
May this hard, horrible Time become no more than dreams

Though a March through Hell is never as simple as it seem

Pony Express

The Pony Express delivered mail when the west was wild
The Riders toted Bibles but weren't real meek or mild
Orphans All They were so none would miss them should one die
But Conditions being what they were it was well worth
Their while to try
Light wiry Boys were what They wanted somewhere in their teens
The Bosses tried to get them to keep both body and mind fairly clean
Bugles were issued to each boy should They need help
Against Bandits after money or Indians after scalps
They carried Colt revolvers with which to protect the mail
If They should be attacked somewhere along the trail
The Riders carried letters and so forth inside oilskin to keep it okay
One Rider would meet another, They would trade and both go away
So the Mail was passed between Saint Joseph and the west coast
They claimed They could deliver inside five days
which was no idle boast
Soon the Telegraph Lines were running every which-a-way
Then It was pretty much the End the Pony Express had had its' day
Names of a few of them became famous and went down in History
But Most just punched Cattle not worrying about what could be

A Respectable Man: Captain Abiel Lovejoy of Sidney, ME

Hear now of Captain Abiel Lovejoy, a gentleman most worthy
He married Mary Brown, a buxom Charlestown beauty
Nathaniel, her father was a tavern keeper of decided Tory bent
Which Fact did follow Abiel in the revolution wherever he was sent
Hezekiah, Abiel`s papa was disgraced for loving his strong drink
He in the doghouse the Church did keep
The Church stood by his wife Hannah Austin and their children all
Abiel salvaged the family reputation years after their father`s fall
He and Mary moved to Maine and prospered, had a family and money
too
A well considered Man who served his town and state
Serving on Maine`s first postal commission in his time and date
He and wife Mary were painted by Copley, a artist of note
Abiel captained ships that to Portland, Boston and Jamaica did float
Twice seated in the Massachusetts Legislature he knew tragedy as
well
One Son, Francis was deaf and dumb his case was researched by
Alexander Bell
Captain Abiel lived in Pownalborough, later Sidney too
Eighteen hundred eleven was the last year on earth he viewed

For My Grandmother's Hundredth Birthday

Today you are you are a hundred and what a time it's been
Since you sat on Aunt Rilla's lap and since first you made a friend.
That trip to Stockton Springs in that Park-Overland was really quite a thrill
In spite of all the dust as it went down every hill.
There were good times as well as sad, however brief they were.
Picking berries, eating melons, some quite good stories told and heard.
You grew up and married Arthur Cummings so very long ago
He was more of a hand to talk and peddle instead of reap and sow
You had two beloved children in spite of the hard times and the strife
Time Fraught with worry, the bane of life
So Many doctors: Newcomb, Sally Simpson and Jewell,
Wagner, Grossman and Webb; none of them has been a fool.
Your children married and started families, then your husband died.
He went to be with God up in the sky
You traveled to Virginia to live with Aunt Rena, but you soon returned.
You took care of others' children; one of life's lessons long since learned
You loved to play bingo at the fair in Jackson, and always watched the news on Channel Five.
Little did anyone suspect how great trouble you'd have with your eyes.
Sorrow came, but twice hurt more than most as your children joined the heavenly host.

Yet life continued, happy times and sad to be savored and endured,
the good and the bad.

Advice to Drug Users

Pot, Cocaine, Smack and Crack
Their Users complain they get too much flack
Blindness, Coma, Insanity, Death
That may be in store for those who use that mess
As for the big Dealers I say: "Hang 'em high"
Spread Far and wide the Reason why
Now You dopes who think you must use dope
Please Fight to quit it quick while there still is hope
There's no good Excuse to steal, murder or mug
You can do better without the drugs
Even If You've half fried your brain it could only get worse
You could well end up in the back of a hearse
You might ask "What do I have to live for?"
I don't know What awaits Us beyond Death's door
"I can't take it, just leave me alone" You say
I wish I knew what to say to make You want to stay
Things can hope to get better should you decide to try
If You decide to live We'll help you; Decide to die, We'll cry

The Worth of Things

How much is Anything in this world worth?
That that is precious in One's eyes in Another's there's nothing worse
The most precious things We have we frequently forget
Until Something comes and offers them a threat
The Air which we breathe, the Ground on which we walk
The Food which We are able to eat; Our Ability to talk
The Fact that people care what happens to us
Yet Continually We gripe and fuss
That We can't anywhere near make both ends meet
Though We've got some sort of shelter not live out in the street
While We have to scrimp and save We don't starve by any means
More is Nice, I quite agree, but far better than nothing to have times
lean
We may not have the key to every door
But Think of All You have when you think yourself poor

A Cowboy's Letter

Dear Mama, You had me in the middle of the plain
Since then I guess I give you nothing but pain
You always wanted me to be a Lawyer or some such
But I like herding cattle and for me that's enough
You wanted Me to be a Gentleman, but I'm a cowboy instead
Though I ain't real respected I 'bout always do get fed
Mama, I'm sorry if I hurt you by being what I am
Things changed a mite for me when I fought the Rebs for Uncle Sam
We're getting ready to drive some cows up Colonel Goodnight's trail
Clear on up to Kansas City where there is a rail
I'm Riding for a Colonel Claybourne who owns the Circle C
Outfit's mostly Rebs but Pay is plenty good to me
When We get paid I'll likely spend down to my last dollar
Then I'll likely spend a spell in jail and think of you, sweet Mama
Fellar told Me once Life is something We should all enjoy
Mama, I'm Sorry but I'm Happy too; signed - Your Son, the Cowboy

The Mother's Letter to the Cowboy

My dearest Son, it has been so long
The Wondering about You was a worrisome thorn
That You chose not to be a lawyer matters not at all
Though I pray You won't break your neck in a fall
I also hope that living among those ruffians won't get you shot or hung
It is Fine by me if you choose to rope and ride and shovel dung
I hope Mr Claybourne is a gentleman who'll deal fair and true
That He'll not cheat you of your wages else do worse things to you
Jeremiah, your cousin Jethro told us all of the wound
You suffered at Shiloh
Thank God, It didn't start to turn gangerous
like your poor brother Philo's
Aunt Lucretia and Elizabeth got out of Gettysburg all right
Though They lost their home in that terrible fight
Granpa Benjamin Mc Culloch died that day You may know
The old Fool took his rifle and hobbled out, it's said but He was just
too slow
You know his mind was going, He thought He was sixteen
It was a mercy to him really, His Mind used to be so keen
For him the Enemy wore red coats instead of ones of gray
More and more each day back to 1812 his mind would stray
We are proud of how well You bore the McCulloch part during the War
You, and Jethro, poor Philo, James, John and Christopher
Jeremiah, your Father would be proud of You as well

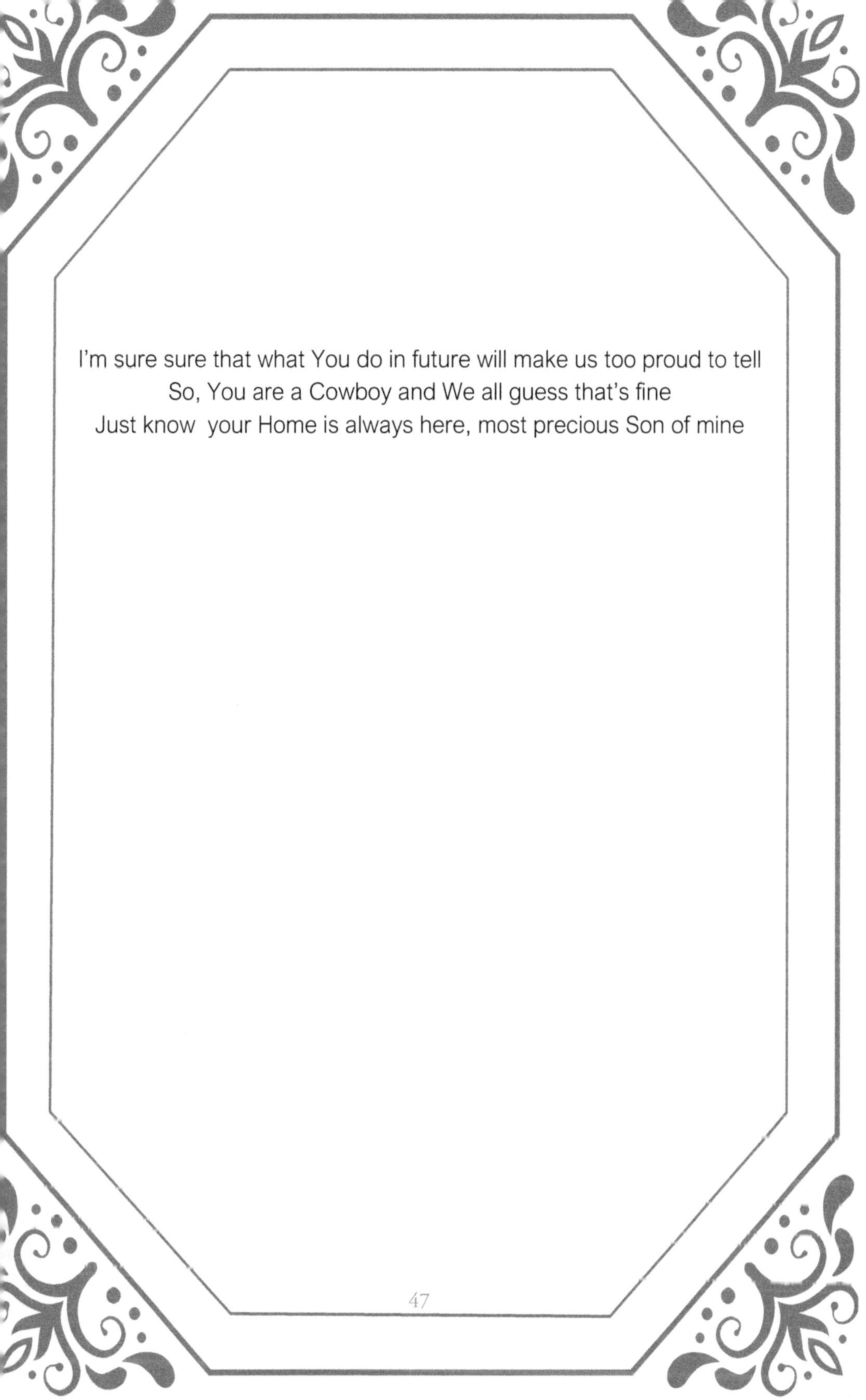

I'm sure sure that what You do in future will make us too proud to tell
So, You are a Cowboy and We all guess that's fine
Just know your Home is always here, most precious Son of mine

Thanks for Giving

Thanks for giving, Lord to Us the breath of life
Thanks for giving Mercy when forbidden fruit We kiefed
Thanks for giving us a second chance beyond the Flood
Thanks for giving us both Souls and blood
Thanks for giving us free will
Thanks for giving us the choice between good and ill
Thanks for giving us the Moon, Sun, darkness and day
Thanks for giving us Someone to show Us the way
Thanks for giving us your Son to our punishment bear
Thanks for giving us the right to care
Thanks for giving us hope and last but not least
Thanks for giving us bounty to have this feast

Passage to a New Life

What I knew has passed life begins anew
Employment is gone got to find a new job to do
I'll tender loyalty to another and hope all comes out all right
I'll try to keep an open mind, turn darkness into daylight
Ignore fear of rejection and not being up to snuff
I hope better things will come after all this stuff
Time may be on my side if only for the moment
I Believe I'll like this place to which fate has me sent
If I believe strongly enough perhaps I can make it so
For the old life has ebbed and does not exist anymore

Hunter's Morning

One day in mid November He got off from work
He got dressed in the dark, misbuttoned his shirt
He donned his orange cap and zipped up his orange coat
He went out with his rifle, eyes searching, full of hope
He crept out slow fifteen minutes before dawn
Trying to get that Buck that had been feeding on the lawn
The Deer's head came up, in a flash he was gone
The young Man followed into the woods, then the chase was on
The Deer ran faster than the young man aimed
That time He didn't hit him, would the next time be the same?
The Hunter looked carefully about him as He went into the wood
He was alert and careful as He hoped the other hunters would be as
they should
There were dry Leaves and little vegetation showed
No wonder Hunters yearn for a little snow
He took care not to trip, not to shoot himself or another
He moved slowly through the brush although it seemed a bother
There was the Buck off to the right
He aimed carefully, it was after daylight
The Bullet connected, the Buck went down
Kicking and thrashing upon the ground
He got out his knife and finished the work
He was careful not to mess up and cause the deer more hurt
Hunting is necessary to keep the numbers few
I'm glad He did what some have to do

The Battle of Hampden, Maine
(September 1814)

They came down from ruined Bangor, Some of Britain's favored sons
Some of Whom may have fought the French with Wellington
The Farmer's miltia was badly outmatched and but poorly drilled
If They had stood up to the onslaught most likely allwould have been
killed
As the Lobsterbacks marched into Hampden the farmers ran and hid
The Miltiamen took but few shots as they did
In the Course of the Incident two British soldiers lay dead
They were buried by the locals when all had been done and said
The Redcoats went from house to house, breaking down the doors
Even as the Farmers retreated into the woods and moors
They headed out toward Newburgh, Dixmont and Monroe
The Families grabbing up all their possessions from livestock to hoes
The Farmers marched quickly as the musicians sounded the retreat
They were embarrassed at the ease with which the British accomplished
their defeat
The Miltia's General Blake was scorned for his prudent action
Nearly being chased out of Hampden by a certain faction
He went to Brewer, dying there an old, old man
People came to almost realize why He had failed to make a stand
Not Cowardice but prudence elicited his decision
If They had stood and fought the Redcoats would soon have wiped
out the division

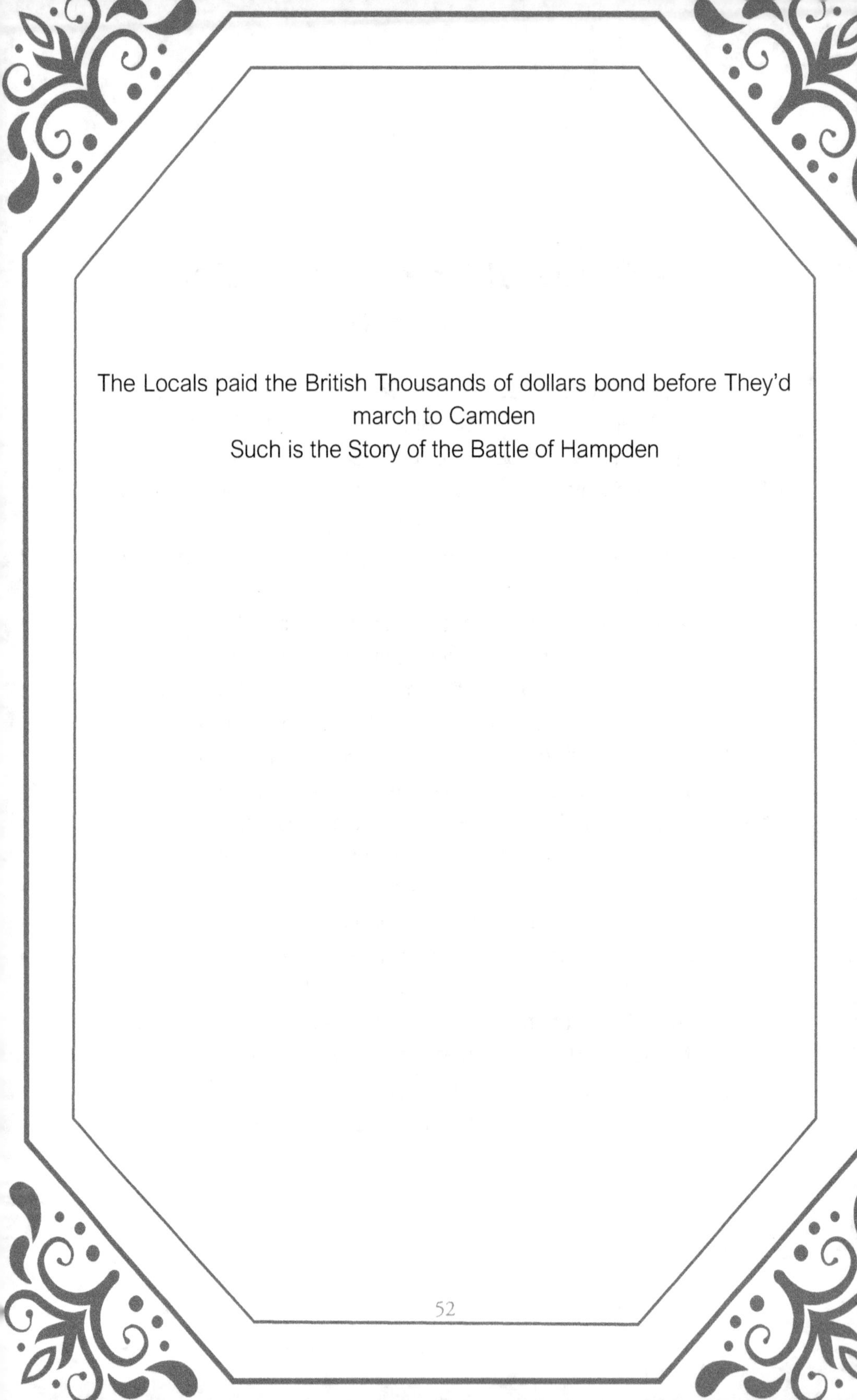
The Locals paid the British Thousands of dollars bond before They'd march to Camden
Such is the Story of the Battle of Hampden

You Think You've Got the Right?

You think you've got the right to smack a woman up side her head?
That you can kick one in the corner or beat one till she's half dead?
You say you can't help it, she makes you act that way
You do it and I hope you get a taste one day
Probably in a jail with a two hundred odd pound brute
Just because something of your looks does not him suit
Doesn't sound so good when it could happen to you
Imagine if such horror were really coming true
So think twice before you do it again
Then suddenly discover you no longer have a friend
Not one to help you through it all
No one who will heed your call

Master Stephen Hopkins

To Master Stephen Hopkins who longed for this new land
Years before the Mayflower docked off Plymouth strand
A high tempered Man who quested after adventure
With Means enough to have two young men in his indenture
Besides a Cabin for himself and his immediate company
He greatly disliked London, wanting somewhere more free
By contrast his daughter Constance for that city long did long
Annoying her Father by daydreaming and sitting looking forlorn
The Hopkinses at length joined the Pilgrims' religious way
Stephen not wishing his family from Christianity to sway
While not of their Faith He strove to be heard
He was made an assistant Governor as people listened to his word
To his house first came the sagamore Samoset
Overtures of Friendship were exchanged that first time that They met
His Family settled Eastham and there his son Gyles Katherine
Wheldon to wife took
They had many children including Deborah who wed Josiah Cook
Many are the Families that can deduce at least one descent from him
Indeed there are several lines which have grown all too dim
A Man of Intelligence who remained prosperous until He died at the
age of sixty-one
There's little more to be said, I guess this poem's done

Would You?

What would you do if you had a chance to 'do-over' your life?
If you have never married would you take a husband or wife?
Would you strive to do those things for which you strive
Else set off down another road and see where you arrive
Would you remain at home or go off far away
Try your hand in a different spot, find a different way
Would you bring to fruitation things you let wither and die?
Stay on that course you didn't give a better try
Would you be religious or stand up for the rights of man?
Would you fight against those injustices that crop up in your land?
Yet, what of those choices you do not choose yourself?
The ones that happen which you cannot help
Things coming to an end you have no power to influence
Decisions that are made which may or not make sense

The Brothers Maguire

Two Boys went out from Mercer one fine October day
Hosea and William Maguire lied to join up They say
Seventeen and Fifteen not Nineteen and eighteen their ages were
But the Army took many youths fresh out of school
Abe Lincoln called forth our sons to war on Men in gray
Boys fresh out of fields where They cut and stored up hay
The Twenty-fourth Infantry joined the conflict in 'sixty-two
An Enlistment these Boys did not voluntarily eschew
Hosea was mustered out, disabled by January of 'Sixty-three
Young William gave up his life in hope that all Men should be free It
was not new, this wish for liberation
At fifteen their Great Grandpa took part in the forming of our nation
So much young blood, early hardened sacrifice
Men before quite time, what paltry honor We can give must suffice

A Fisherman's Day

White capped Waves rush through great rocks
Down the shore the Boats are docked
The Fishermen prepare for another busy day
Soon the Schooners are headed out away from the quay
They go forth to toss their nets into the sea
They catch fish to sell to you and me
Today They are lucky for the sea is calm
There should be less chance that Someone will come to harm
Only Fools and desperate Men go out when the Sea is really rough
Some Young Men trying to prove they're tough
"Stay Home rough Days, young Men and secure your boats"
Maybe You'll yet live to be old goats

The Country Singer

He took his guitar from its' battered case
He got up on stage his audience to face
He sings about the trouble He's had on the way
He hopes and prays success will come and stay
His Heroes these days are Jackson and Strait
This Country Boy from New York state
He went off to college, got a MBA
Something He's not using today
His Girlfriend left when He quit work
He bought him a Stetson and western shirt
Now He strums tunes on his worn guitar
Feels fulfilled when He does, here's where his friends are
In this cruel uncertain world He may one day have a hit
But now He enjoys what he loves just being a part of it

The Two Fishermen

The gray-haired Man was decked out with waders, rod and reel
He was wearing a Life vest and Gilligan hat seeking what water
concealed
He was prepared as always with extra rods, hooks and line
For every Eventuality for which He could divine
A Teen walked beside the brook and settled on the bank
Wearing only bermuda shorts, his form was long and lank
He held an alder stick, string tied to its' end
He had a nut and hook tied to the other with bait from a friend
He plunked It in the water and fish were on his line
The Man in the brook stood waiting, expectant everything was fine
The Kid was landing fish, tossing them back inside
The Man was getting impatient 'No Fish' this He couldn't abide
"You're scaring the fish, get outta here!" the Man mouthed at the Kid
The Kid chuckled, shrugging as his Old Man blew his lid
"Dad, I don't know why I'm getting what You wish
I just catch and throw them back, 'cause I really don't like fish"

Vision of the Maine Coast

Brown green Waves caress a shore
Beach of black mud has a odd allure
It gives way to Rocks of hard stone
A place and a feeling for One alone
Big white Gulls hover and dive
To gain Carrion or Prey dead or alive
Here`s to the Place, the People who love it most
All Year Inhabitants of the State of Maine coast
They who dig in the mud of the black clam flats
They who rake the fields where bueberries are at
Those who toil with traps in love with the sea
Despite all Its` tumultuousness, All that is and shall be
Fishermen, Guides, Restaurants and Keepers of Tourist shops
Where People who have money like to stay and shop
Hardworking Tradesmen and Harvesters of the ocean
Stop and see It all the grand display put on
We love that you love Maine and all its` wealth we share
Please Remember and be generous when you do shop there

Mortimer the Christmas ball

Mortimer the Christmas ball had a shiny silvered face
With one red stripe around the middle in just the right place
The Bensons, a young couple bought him before one Christmas Day
They had a kitten Tiger who so did love to play
Sly Kitty knocked Mortimer off the tree and rolled him around the floor
In under the Range that stood beneath the cupboard doors.
In the dim half- light he lay dreaming of the tree
Those deep green boughs where He`d been nestled for everyone to see
He saw the blinking brightly colored rays of light
While the Bensons commemorated the birth of the Savior one long ago night
Time passes, He isn`t found, that tree and others are taken down
He`s grimy, covered in dust while outside he hears many sounds
Crying Babies, laughing children, anger, pleasure and smiles
Life is flowing there rocky mile by rocky mile
The Bensons are no longer young time has turned their hair to gray
One Day They decide to sell their house and move away
They get their son to move the range and examine the floor
When That was done Mortimer was found to be sure
Grime caked his face Time faded paint until his looks were gone
"What`s This, Mom?" the Son asked : " An Ornament from before Iwas born?"
Mrs Benson sighed and nodded recalling that Christmas Eve.
"Sole Survivor. I guess the Cat batted it off the tree."

The Son said: " Well, I`ll clean it up, Ginny`ll paint it and we can hang
it on our tree this year"
"Sure" Mr Benson grumbled: " Set never was the same.
the Rest are in the closet in the box in which they came."
"What`s that, Dear? "Mrs Benson asks. Mr Benson looks uncomfortable
at that.
"There were two sets, dear, remember? He said: "I hid the rest away
to keep them from that cat."

Christmas rolled around and Mortimer had been restored
He hung with his fellow ornaments many years more
The Cycle continued on, Year after year he saw the light of day
With the Cats, the Dogs and children He likes things better that way

Meditation

Almighty God this now I pray
For Patience and Courage to carry me through every day
Give Me Compassion for those in need
And the Will to transform the thought into deed
Lord, You know well I have the best of intentions
Yet Somehow I fail to give them greater dimensions
Why do I doubt anything I have to give?
Perhaps even the courage to really live
Perhaps I`ll yet strike the right chord at the right time
Then All that I wish for may come to be mine
Maybe I`m a greedy fool that I hope for all
From That great a height would be a hard fall
I know not where I fit into your great plan
Yet maybe `ere I die I shall do something for man
Maybe I`ll not have greatness for myself but help another to find their
way
That hard Path to save us from Evil`s dark sway

State of Grace

When London bridge has fallen down and blood and wealth don`t
matter
When All is Calm and warm and bright and Future is the latter
When All may enjoy all they care to enjoy yet not hurt one another
When No one Believes that for any reason they are better than the
other
When Peace on Earth and Mercy for all are the order of the day
When It doesn`t matter if this is the End of Days
When the Sound of joy fills the world and all have enough to survive
Then We`ll know the Secrets and al shall be alive
Approach God with humble heart and in the kingdom you will thrive
Love Others more than you do yourself then will you be forever live.

www.ingramcontent.com/pod-product-compliance
Lightning Source LLC
Chambersburg PA
CBHW071206300726
48975CB00004B/1303